GROSS AND DISGUSTING THINGS

GROSS AND DISGUSTING FOOD

A Crabtree Branches Book

Julie K. Lundgren

Crabtree Publishing
crabtreebooks.com

School-to-Home Support for Caregivers and Teachers

This high-interest book is designed to motivate striving students with engaging topics while building fluency, vocabulary, and an interest in reading. Here are a few questions and activities to help the reader build upon his or her comprehension skills.

Before Reading:

- *What do I think this book is about?*
- *What do I know about this topic?*
- *What do I want to learn about this topic?*
- *Why am I reading this book?*

During Reading:

- *I wonder why...*
- *I'm curious to know...*
- *How is this like something I already know?*
- *What have I learned so far?*

After Reading:

- *What was the author trying to teach me?*
- *What are some details?*
- *How did the photographs and captions help me understand more?*
- *Read the book again and look for the vocabulary words.*
- *What questions do I still have?*

Extension Activities:

- *What was your favorite part of the book? Write a paragraph on it.*
- *Draw a picture of your favorite thing you learned from the book.*

TABLE OF CONTENTS

FIRE UP YOUR TASTEBUDS

Hungry people all over the world eat all kinds of foods. Some might have you reaching for a fork, while others might make you gag.

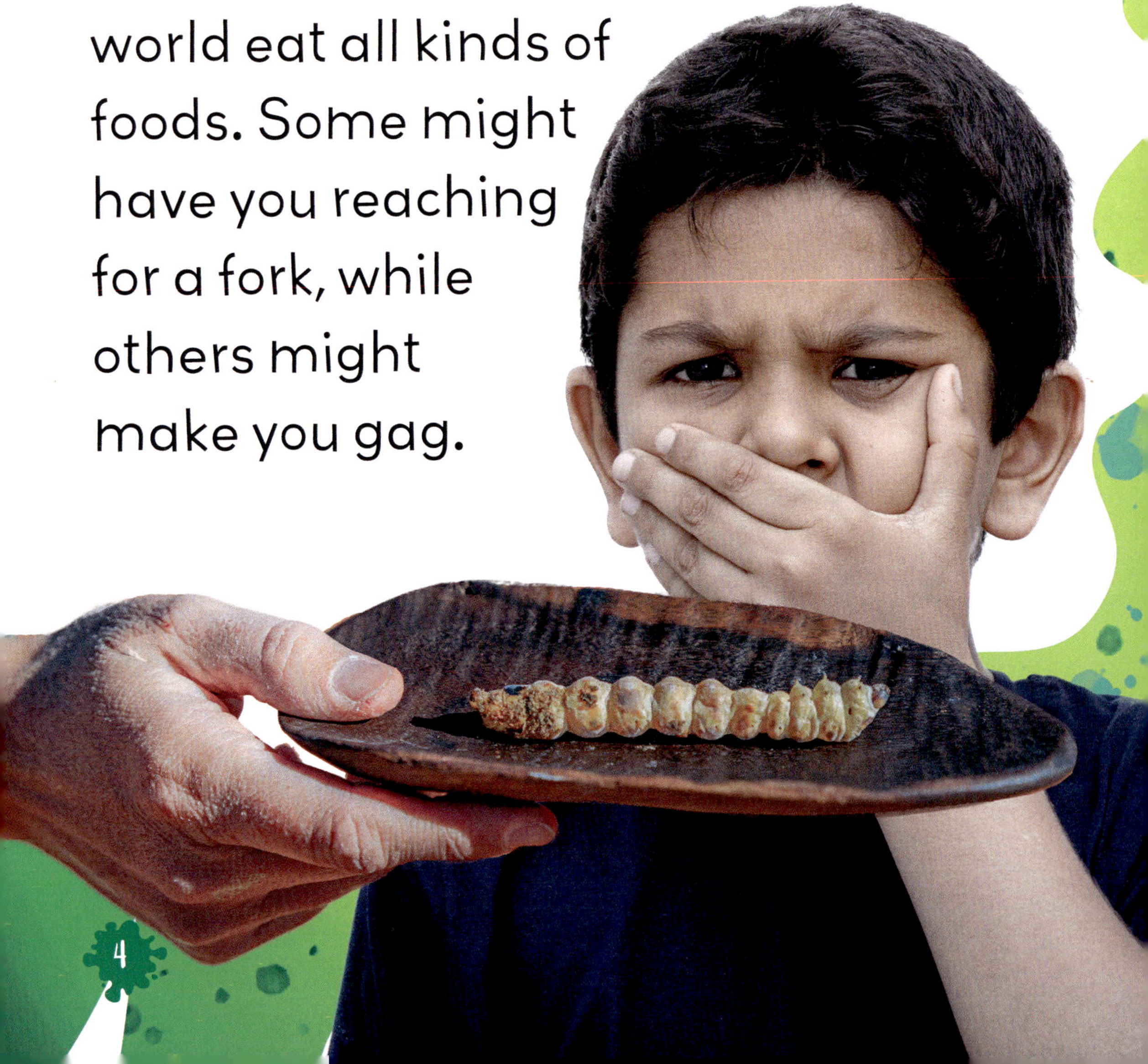

Jellied eels have strong flavor and a dramatic look.

Fork or Puke?

Meaty witchetty grubs from Australia taste like almonds and have crispy skin.

At the Disgusting Food Museum, visitors explore the purpose of disgust, eat strange foods, and learn more about how foods and cultures go together. Every visitor gets a barf bag with their entry ticket.

While the feeling of disgust can protect us from eating something bad for us, it's okay to open your mind, and your mouth, to new foods. Here we go!

Dancing squid is served alive.

GUTS, BRAINS, AND BODY PARTS

Wise and practical people use every part of an animal. Pig farmers sometimes say they use everything but the squeal.

Black pudding contains pig blood, oatmeal, and pork fat.

I'm Not a Vampire, You're a Vampire

A rich soup from Poland contains dried fruits, cream, spices, a duck, and its blood.

Nothing like a crispy fritter to put crunch in your sandwich. Would you dare to eat one made of sheep brain? A little squeeze of lemon perks it right up.

Sheep brain tastes a little like scrambled eggs.

Fork or Puke?

Head cheese is not cheese at all. It's a loaf of the meat, tongue, fat, gelatin, and broth from a whole pig head, minus the brains.

Maybe brains are not for you. Intestines can be cleaned and cooked, or stuffed with salted, chopped, or ground meat for sausage.

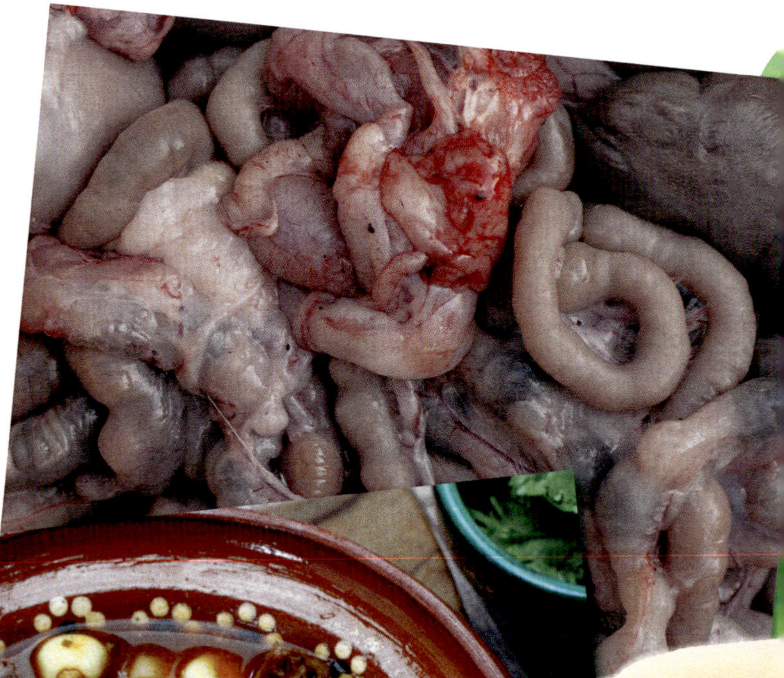

Stomachs make special soups like menudo.

Haggis

Fork or Puke?

Do you have the stomach for haggis? To prepare, stuff a sheep stomach with chopped, spiced heart, lungs, liver, oatmeal, and fat.

Cooked cow stomach

Nothing warms quite like a bowl of soup. As you give it a stir, a whole eyeball floats to the surface. Fish eyes add extra flavor and a gooey texture.

The fish in a hearty stargazy pie stare right back at you.

Fork or Puke?

In Vietnam, imagine being served a beating cobra heart.

BREAKFAST, ANYONE?

To start the day, coffee and pancakes hit the spot. Palm civets eat coffee cherries and poop the seeds. People collect, clean, and roast the seeds to make one of the world's most expensive coffees. Pair that with some blood pancakes topped with jam!

LUWAK COFFEE

The five-second rule does not apply to civet droppings.

Hard no on blood pancakes? Top toast with beet jelly, Marmite, or caviar! Serve alongside a whole egg with the bird and yolk inside!

Caviar, or fish eggs, pop in your mouth.

How do you like your eggs?

Taste This

Marmite is a salty yeast paste leftover after making beer.

STOP THE ROT

For thousands of years, people have pickled food as a way to stop it from rotting. Food is soaked in a brine made of salt, vinegar, water, and spices.

Pickled cucumbers taste great on a burger, but how about pickled pigs' feet?

Sweet and Sour

Flavor your next batch of cupcakes with pickle juice, chopped pickles, and dill frosting! Top with a pickle slice to finish your fun but strange treat.

Fermentation also saves food for later. Ancient Romans packed fish blood, guts, and gills in a pot in the sun with lots of salt for several months. Fermented fish sauce makes a change from ketchup!

A form of the Roman fish sauce is still made today, and cats are thankful!

Some countries outlaw certain foods. Bacteria, mites, and larvae in some cheeses may cause serious illness. Because of its stench, durian fruit may not be allowed on public transportation.

Durian fruit

After they are dug up, the sharks are cut and hung to try.

Not Against the Law: Buried Shark

In Iceland, people bury a whole shark for several months to get rid of the terrible ammonia taste. Then they cut and dry it.

This rare cheese crawls with insect larvae.

SNACKS AND DESSERTS FOR THE BRAVE

Still hungry? Candy, snacks, and special desserts await! Would you eat an ice cream made of reindeer fat, berries, and snow?

People eat roasted crickets like popcorn!

Bug Bites

Crunch into roasted ants and grasshoppers dipped in chocolate. Lick a lollipop containing a whole insect!

Foods are tied to their lands and people, and the need to eat. Hunger seems to find a way to make any available resource into food. What are you hungry for?

Grilled scorpion or deep-fried tarantula are common snacks in parts of the world.

Brush and Floss

Is that an insect leg caught between your teeth?

GLOSSARY

ammonia (uh-MOH-nyee-uh): A waste product with a strong smell

bacteria (back-TEER-ee-uh): Tiny living things that break down food, and may cause illness

brine (BRYNE): A liquid of salt and vinegar used for pickling food

caviar (KAV-ee-ar): The pickled eggs from certain fish, like salmon and sturgeon

fermentation (fur-min-TAY-shun): A process by which bacteria and other tiny living things break down food

gelatin (JELL-uh-tin): A clear jelly made from animal skin, bones, horns, and hoofs

intestines (in-TES-tinz): The part of the digestive system after the stomach where nutrients are absorbed by the body

larvae (LAR-vee): In insects, the stage of development between egg and adult

palm civets (PAHM SIV-its): Small, forest animals in Asia that are active at night, eating fruit, insects, and mice

wichetty grubs (WICH-uh-tee GRUBZ): Larvae of certain moths in Australia

INDEX

WEBSITES TO VISIT

https://disgustingfoodmuseum.com

https://kidworldcitizen.org/category/food/

www.tasteatlas.com

ABOUT THE AUTHOR

Julie K. Lundgren

Julie K. Lundgren grew up on the north shore of Lake Superior, a place of woods, water, and adventure. She loves bees, dragonflies, old trees, and science and has a special place in her heart for disgustingly cool animals. Her interests led her to a degree in biology and a lifelong curiosity about wild places.

Crabtree Publishing

crabtreebooks.com 800-387-7650

Produced by: Blue Door Education for Crabtree Publishing
Written by: Julie K. Lundgren
Designed by: Jennifer Dydyk
Edited by: Tracy Nelson Maurer
Proofreader: Crystal Sikkens
Production manager: Candice Campbell

Hardcover	978-1-4271-5447-7
Paperback	978-1-4271-5453-8
Ebook (pdf)	978-1-4271-5459-0
Epub	978-1-4271-5465-1
Read-along	978-1-4271-5471-2
Audio book	978-1-4271-5477-4

Printed in the U.S.A./CP082026

Library and Archives Canada Cataloguing in Publication

Title: Gross and disgusting food / Julie K. Lundgren.
Names: Lundgren, Julie K., author.
Description: Series statement: Gross and disgusting things | "A Crabtree branches book". | Includes index.
Identifiers: Canadiana (print) 20210220422 | Canadiana (ebook) 20210220430 | ISBN 9781427154477 (hardcover) | ISBN 9781427154538 (softcover) | ISBN 9781427154590 (HTML) | ISBN 9781427154651 (EPUB) | ISBN 9781427154712 (read-along ebook)
Subjects: LCSH: Food—Juvenile literature. | LCSH: Food—Miscellanea—Juvenile literature. | LCSH:Food habits—Juvenile literature. | LCSH: Food habits—Miscellanea—Juvenile literature.
Classification: LCC TX355 .L86 2022 | DDC j641.3—dc23

Published in Canada
Crabtree Publishing
616 Welland Avenue
St. Catharines, Ontario
L2M 5V6

Published in the United States
Crabtree Publishing
347 Fifth Avenue
Suite 1402-145
New York, NY 10016

Photographs: Cover photo © sumr Charoen Krung Photography, cover splat art on cover and throughout © SpicyTruffel pg. 4 grub photo © Benny Marty, boy © saisnaps pg. 5 (top) © Monkey Business Images (bottom) © nicemyphoto pg. 6 © (top) trabantos (bottom) © John T Takai pg. 7 squid © yod67 bowl of food © iamlukyeee pg. 8 (top) © Zanna Pesnina (bottom) © TunedIn by Westend61 pg. 9 (top) © Viktor1 (bottom) © Dar1930 duck © NotionPic pg. 10 (top) © NinaM (bottom) Ryzhkov Photography pg. 11 (top) © getcloser (bottom) © AS Food studio pg. 12 (top) © Piotr Velixar (bottom) © bonchan pg. 13 (top) © Philip Kinsey (bottom) © zcw pg. 14 (top) © Davis Dorss (bottom) © Nowaczyk pg. 15 (top) © Dewin ID (bottom) © Irina Kalinina pg. 16 (top) © kajornyot wildlife photography, (bottom) © Galyna_P, pg. 17 (top) © Wisnu Yudowibowo, (bottom) © Tong_stocker, pg. 18 (top) ©Nicole M Iizuka, toast © Pg.Seven, marmite © chrisdorney, pg. 19 © Davisaurus Rex, pg. 20 © plate and jar photo © Warren Price Photography, pig's feet © Krasowit, pg. 21 (top photo) © sarenac77, (bottom) © LightField Studios, pg. 22 © Artsholic, pg. 23 (top) © george photo cm, (bottom) © De Jongh Photography, pg. 24 girl © Krakenimages.com, unpeeled fruit © Davdeka, peeled fruit © gowithstock, pg. 25 (bottom) © Gengis90, pg. 26 © TorresGlz, pg. 27 (top) © PitukTV, (bottom) © aon168, pg. 28 © Jan Jenka, pg. 29 (top) © meunierd, (bottom) © Krakenimages.com. All images from Shutterstock.com except pg. 25 (top) © Chris 73 (Wikipedia) https://creativecommons.org/licenses/by-sa/3.0/deed.en,

Library of Congress Cataloging-in-Publication Data

Names: Lundgren, Julie K., author.
Title: Gross and disgusting food / Julie K. Lundgren.
Description: New York : Crabtree Publishing Company, 2022. | Series: Gross and disgusting things - a Crabtree branches book | Includes bibliographical references and index.
Identifiers: LCCN 2021022337 (print) | LCCN 2021022338 (ebook) | ISBN 9781427154477 (hardcover) | ISBN 9781427154538 (paperback)| ISBN 9781427154590 (ebook) | ISBN 9781427154651 (epub) | ISBN 9781427154712
Subjects: LCSH: Ethnic food--Juvenile literature. | Food habits--Juvenile literature. | Aversion--Juvenile literature.
Classification: LCC TX355 .L94 2022 (print) | LCC TX355 (ebook) | DDC 641.3--dc23
LC record available at https://lccn.loc.gov/2021022337
LC ebook record available at https://lccn.loc.gov/2021022338